T0064517

ZOOFARI

MARIA DAVIS

BALBOA.PRESS

A DIVISION OF HAY HOUSE

Balboa Press books may be ordered through booksellers or by contacting:

Balboa Press
A Division of Hay House
1663 Liberty Drive
Bloomington, IN 47403
www.balboapress.com.au
AU TFN: 1 800 844 925 (Toll Free inside Australia)
AU Local: 0283 107 086 (+61 2 8310 7086 from outside Australia)

Print information available on the last page.

ISBN: 978-1-5043-2166-2 (sc)
ISBN: 978-1-5043-2167-9 (e)

Balboa Press rev. date: 10/20/2020

Welcome to
ZOOFARI!

MARIA DAVIS

By the wayside was a sign!

As the people were approaching the sign reads, Welcome to ZOOFARI.

Peter was explaining, "This place is a wonderful wonderland of all animals."

It is a long walk to the entry gate.

The crowds are walking in long queues moving forwards to the entrance. The kids in the queues were all anticipating a great day in the zoo by showing their enthusiasm for laughter, crying, taunting, and teasing each other.

"How about this weather, it is so fantastic isn't it?" "It is really the best weather ever!" Peter was feeling overwhelmed by the queues of people.

"Great day out for families to walk all about," said Peter.

The Jones family bought their tickets for a group for 2 Adults and 3 young children all under the ages of nine.

"Hey, kids!" "Let's all go to the information desk to collect our maps of the ZOOFARI." Peter their father guided them. Then he smiled in expectation of an enjoyable day.

"Look out yonder to see all animals great and small!" "Oh, what fun it is for us all!" Peter continued to guide his son Charlie by saying.

"Hop on over like a good Skippy do Kangaroo." "Let's have lots of fun as peoples' awesomeness often do," Peter said with a smile. Then Charlie surprised his dad by asking, "Do I get some Skippy points for this too!!?"

"Hey, hey!" Chrissy their elder sister called out to her younger brother, "Little mister charming." "I don't know about you, but I would love to hug a cuddly gray koala rather than try to box with a kangaroo!" Chrissy snuck upon him by hugging Chad!! Chad is her other twin brother. "Hahaha," she laughed as she could not help herself. Chad responded to Chrissy. "Ahhh, I am too big to be squeezed as a koala by the likes of you." "The koalas are a lot smaller size than me, wouldn't you agree?" Charlie got excited and shrugged his shoulder at Chad. He said, "Look out there at that kangaroos which are not ordinarily gray or brown but are reddish in colour and they are also very tall creatures!" "Besides these red kangaroos are much larger stature for boxing rather than any kind of wallabies which are a lot smaller kind of kangaroos." "As we had seen some of them earlier on our way!" Anita, the children's mother commented, "Watch this red kangaroo." "It is so gentle." "The kangaroo is soothing with the twitch and stretching his paw to relieve that itch giving a light rub a tad on the backside." Anita continues to say, "Yes, you have a look in the front of the pouch." "See it?" "A little joey!" "A baby kangaroo seems so comfortably bliss sitting in mother's pouch." Chrissy remarked, "Aww, so adorable!" "Anyhow, Koalas are also small animals and they look a lot sweeter!" Charlie's sudden response came, "But only if you let me cuddle him first?" He winged right on over towards his own twin brother Chad. He extended out his arms suddenly to give him a humongous lift and huggable squeeze taking it too lightly. Charlie went as red as a kangaroo as he could barely lift his brother's weight. Chrissy replied, "I also cuddled that twin gray koala earlier!!!" "Yeah!" "Hahaha," as she laughed.

Moving right along as you do to the next place. The family carries on having a good time and not worried how much time was spent at any one place!

Chad had an odd question for his mother!

"Have you seen a hippy hoppy piteous before?" Their mother was perplexed by Chad's question.

Anita remarked.

"Preposterous?" "I think you meant to say a hippopotamus which is that one that just happened to trot along one side of us?" "Oh my, what large nostrils it has and not a lot of Snuffy Duffy awful us," Anita said jokingly. "I meant to say it has large sniffy nostrils!" as their mother laughed. Someone is as cheeky as their mother was trying to be. A sudden need for Chad to sneeze on her. Anita said to Chad, "Cover your nose when you sneeze to show you are polite!"

Charlie laughed at Chad's sneezing gesture!

He stuck his toughest tongue out at Charlie!

"Nah!"

"Well, well Chad your behaviour is incredibly cheeky as a gesture of sneezy." Their mother said. "Well then, here we are with the real big Rhinoceros!" "Yes indeed, it is as large an animal as the Hippopotamus and it has a longish face with a horn on the end of his nose," said Charlie.

"Do Rhinoceros has a sore nose?" Said Chrissy." "Oh, they most certainly don't!", their dad responded. Chrissy nodded her head, "I agree with you daddy as this one has a double spike horn at the end of its nose." Chad said. "Some Rhinos use their horns for their self-defense." "It is a lot different looking from a hippopotamus!" Peter said, "You got that right." "Chad is just a bit strongly opinionated about a strong nose feature," Chad continues to say. "Rhinoceros doesn't resemble any dinosaur of a sore front nose but perhaps resembles a cousin to Triceratops!" Peter said, "Tops!" "Let us carry on forwards as we don't have all day trying to top that." While his father nodded, the family walked over to the next station.

"Hey, look over here!" "These Pandas!" "They originate from the Central Southern part of China," Anita remarked!

Pandas are all about laying on their back swinging side to side holding onto their toes. "Her name is Ping!" Chrissy exclaimed. "She is going around the grounds rolling cheerfully." "Please stop Missy!" Chrissy rolled her eyes all around and said, "I think you missed me Missy." "I am feeling fuzzy watching dizzily." "Pong, the male Panda is eating those long stalks of bamboo shoots." Chrissy continues to say, "Ping suddenly flings up off the bamboo strings which could not stop herself from popping out forwards away!" "Ping is so passionate about those bamboo sprouts!!" "Oh Wah." "What a cutie Panda Ping and Pong as they appear so playful rolling all about on the plains!" Chrissy was holding onto mummy's arm and she said, "Pong is now holding onto those bamboo shoots cuddling a bunch in his arms." "Oh, how adorable are these white and black bears hanging about and laying on their backs all comfortable alike,"

Chrissy is giggling to herself.

"Is there such an animal as big as King Kong in the ZOOFARI?" Chrissy inquired.

Peter said, "How could you think of them in such a way as those grand great gigantic Gorillas?" "Gorillas are gorgeous species and nowadays they are also in danger of extinction!" "Hum, hum."

Their father gestured, "Let's look on towards the giraffes." "Look see, giraffes hidden in between the branches of canopies of tall trees?" Anita said, "These remarkable animals are habitat in Eastern parts of Africa." Peter continued. "Their looks are tall, lean and yellow with brown patches all over their body with a sleek long neck and along with smooth hairline." "They have four skinny long legs too." Giraffes seem astonished by glancing in between branches and leaves with upright stout horns and big brown eyes staring at each other and sticking out their long black tongues between bushy evergreens." "They like to eat carrots too; do you see that!?" Peter said, "Wait, see as one of them is approaching towards me!!" As a giraffe is on its way stretching out his long neck. It lowers his head gliding over Peter while batting his eyelids! "Oh, my what big eyes you have?" "My what a long black tongue you have?" Charlie exclaimed so excitedly. "And I see those stout two horns on its head too." "It is swinging overpass and daddy's sights may miss it as the giraffe carries off away swoosh past Chad's head."

"Chad was glancing at those big bright eyes!" He remarked. "Whoosh and woo hoo!!!" "It is fun and so cool as it swung passed over our heads!!!" Chad tried to extend his arms up high to catch it and missed!! "Ahhhhh!"

"Over on this side of the hills are camels which looks appear so very different from each other!" Anita continues to say, "The camels adapted in the Sahara Desert of Northern Africa." Chrissy said. "One of the camels with one bump and the other has two humps!" "What if it has three hum-pies?" "I guess the camel would be a Pregnant ball?"

"Would that be fair for mummy camel to have big bumpy with three hum-pies!?" Chrissy could not stop asking so many questions. As she went to look up at her mother asking. "Do you think that camels will store up food in one hump and then store up water in the other bump for their travels are on long distant journeys?" Chrissy remarked. Anita was thinking about how her daughter had too many questions and then she told her, "Chrissy you might have to research on that topic for yourself as you are a bright young girl." Chrissy says while smiling at mother, "Thanks mom."

"These four elephants are gorgeous animals." "They are interesting looking in that they also have huge ears too!" "Their origin comes from Africa!!", Peter said.

"The better they can hear us coming from away far over there?" Charlie said with a smile. "I just wonder how do elephants kiss?" Chad said.

"Why certainly, behind the wildest widest bushes." Charlie said, "so surprisingly!?" Chad asked. "Does Tarzan from the movies also run off with the elephants charging forwards with their long tusks using them as a taxi lift running off into the Wild West?" Chrissy laughed with Charlie looking at

Chad with his funny question! Peter quickly replied by saying, "Give it a rest with the rest of the Wildest of the west." "I say you children all have read too many books these days!!" "Anyways these elephants are really wonderful enormous animals, wouldn't you agree with me!?" Peter said. "It is this way the elephants go off into the widest wildest jungles of Africa as they packed up in travels holding trunks up with the tie of the tail in single file." "Couldn't you have just imagine that in my way?!" They all nodded in agreement. Peter continued to say, "These enormous animals stay close together in family herds." "In that way they migrate looking for water and they never forget their family tree!!" "Oh, how wonderful that really is because in that way elephants find not to forget where they came from!" Peter marvelled at the large elephants as their minds forget me not!

Anita was reading silently to herself. "Meerkat inhabit the Kalahari Desert of Botswana in Africa."

"Look over here and let us look over there!" Chad said. "Where?" Charlie asked. "It is the family of marvellous meerkat," Chad exclaimed! "Who?" "Them lot!" Charlie said! "Say I see some of them drop into the ground holes then pop up out over the sandy hillside too," Chad said! "It is a lot like musical notes to pop goes a weasel theme song." "Now look at the both of you jumping up and dropping down as they are mimicking those others too and we are looking at these confusing two," Anita said and Peter winked. "You lot of merry Kats mirror me and so I also mirror you too!!" Peter laughed, "Hahahaha." Charlie laughed at Chad as he chose to leer over at the family meerkat then gave a wave and jumped up then suddenly ducked down! In a loud voice, "STAND at attention please and don't tease!" Their dad said cheerfully.

"Wow!" "What a majestic big animal it really is!" Anita raised her voice! "My goodness, a gorgeous gorilla!" "His bushy black hair is everywhere all around his body." "He has snooty looks to good and proud to carry on!" "This gorilla is an enormous animal," Peter said. "His name is Gregarious." Anita said. Chrissy interrupted. "He is so very black and hairy, looks almost scary!" Then Charlie said, "Ugh, can we move on now?!" Anita ignored Charlie as she continued to say, "His dark looks are so proud handsome and glorious and not so notorious." "What!" "You're kidding me mom!", said Charlie. A female gorilla was nearby. "Wow, his sweet girl mate called Frieda who is not so shy to look over at him." Charlie said, "Frieda is glancing at his grooming habits all over again!" Anita marvelled at the female mate. She was suddenly distracted by watching her children. "Honestly, cut it out Chrissy and Charlie!" Anita started to raise her voice, "The way the both of you carry about by you pulling on your sister's hair as though you did not even care." "Stop pushing over towards Chrissy." Gregarious suddenly stood anxious with a pout to beat his chest out. "Such a very proud look." "He meant to frighten our two boys and our daughter

Chrissy with his frantic dismount." Anita said, "And now look at Frieda as she poked her first on her mate Gregarious." Then Chrissy says, "I dare to say a little more information of a mean pout that could make me shout out!!" "Oh, really," Chrissy sighed "Quickly, let's jump out!!!" Charlie shouts, "Ahhh, ohhhh, ahhh," and he leaped up and jumped out and off he went far away from our sights. "That Gorilla is my favourite animal so far!" Anita remarked! "Exceptionally, well stout." "He is gorgeous Gregarious is not so precarious!"

"These monkeys are black and white with ringed striped tails which are remarkably too long for its special kind," Peter said. "These lemurs were swinging up through the air as their long strong legs help them to leap effortlessly from tree to tree." The one in front jumped on the ground and bounced balletic in leaps along the forward fronts as far off distance right over to the other side. We watched them mesmerized how the Lemur leaped sideward. They climbed up the tree so hurriedly as it started to munch on some leaves. Anita laughed as it sounds as though it giggles whilst munching on their food. "These could be of a different kind of monkeys," said Chrissy. Soon after a younger one followed through the field catching up to cradle upon the mother's back whilst the lemur was eating some fruits laid there as it was prepared for them. Peter replied, "Look how cute that little one is!" "Where did all these monkeys come from?" Chad asked! "Who knows???" Charlie asked! "These Lemurs, OU, OU, OU, are mammals which come only native to the Island of Madagascar and are one of 100 different species of the whee, really whole whee, big Lemur family," Chrissy exclaimed it. "Yes, I know that you read the sign so carefully!" "I feel as though my family are one of a kind too!" Peter remarked to his daughter Chrissy so thoughtfully!

"OI, OI, OI, there is a sign that says, Ostrich's name is Ollie." Charlie exclaimed. "My goodness, are you sure it's not Molly?" Chrissy said. "The M letter is missing in front of Ollie!!" Chrissy says, "lol!"

"She is a loveliest largest fluffy bird I have ever seen." Said Chrissy

"Ollie Ostrich." "She is a really tall bird with a long skinny neck, round full-bodied and long strong legs but she cannot fly?" Peter asked, "Ask the big bird why she cannot fly?" Chrissy glanced over at Charlie for any answer. She continued to say, "She bats her eyelids as she secretly knows she can far out run her neighbour Ernie the Cassowary bird who is staying nearby next door to her!" Charlie continues to say! "Don't be fooled by Ernie's big brown bump on his head and the red-crested neck." "Oh yeah is it called a horned head?" Chad exclaimed. He asks his brother, "Does Ernie's face look naturally blue too?!!" Suddenly Charlie makes unusual sounds. "Gobble, gobble, gobble, gobble!!!" Their mother replied, "That is Charlie again!"

"What?" "My goodness!" "This bird is not a turkey!" "It is called a Cassowary!!" Said Anita! "It kicks out so dangerously as his feet flicks out alike ninjas style!" Chad shouted to Charlie. "Look at me," Chad was jumping foolishly getting out of Charlie's way! Chrissy said to her dad, "Ernie's looks will amuse you as Cassowaries often do?" "What a funny answer!!" Her father replied whilst watching Chad's jumping outstanding actions.

A Peacock bird appears of a bright blue body with a bright green gorgeous long tail of extensions long feathery trail. They originate from Asian countries. The peacock unfolds a full fan showing off his handsome great dome of feathers. It roves around its display of patterned spotted feathers as a playful array of shimmering waves of colours. "Shivers." "Watch him as he fashionably turns slowly about showing off his dome and above the head a fanciful comb of feathers," Anita said. "He finds his happiness looking for his first mate." Nearby a genuine white princess peahen bird that fancies a dance nearby. "She is catching a glance of him in her eyes." Peter marvels listening to Anita speaking. "This female peahen is really a shy bird prancing an uncontrollably dance all on her own!" "She is his biggest fan in all the aviary palace pan," Anita exclaimed, the others smiled.

Anita says to Peter, "See all those tall sleek birds?" "Yes, Peter says, "I love those particular Flamingos whose funny toes goes about dancing a Flamenco and the Tango!" Anita continues to describe them, "They have pretty pinkish feathers." "These birds have longish thin legs which paddle out forwards, outwards and backward just as dancing couples do." Peter nods at Anita as he gazes into her eyes to tell his wife. "Yes, they mingle together having the motion of paddling legs as a Flamenco do dah that bends then sway so carried away." Peter continues to hold her hand saying it affectionately, "Yes Anita I know a pretty Flamingo when I see one!"

Anita replies, "Surely, it's Lady luck to duck out of the way!" She then said, "I also think, these pretty wildlife Flamingos from far off places such as these are mesmerizing to look at from afar too!" "Their lovely feature feathers would look so pretty in the pink, orange, or red dance dos!" Peter implies, "You are feeling romantic notions and you are not even near any oceans my dear?" He quietly chuckles leaned his head into Anita's shoulder and put his arm around her to show off his affectionate approval.

Glistening green shiny sheen are the palms that sway in a wayward wind. Look up hiding there are that lovely pair of toucans that sat perched together on a branch. Toucans are a native to South America, Mexico and the Caribbean where they are in particularly warmer climate places of the rain forests. Their colours are the most striking features. Their beaks appear in a range of colours from beautifully bright yellow, orange, green, or blue. "The bright multiple colours of the largest bird variety is called The Toco Toucans." Peter says, "Toucans look from left yet they look onto their right these toucans do look on from one side." Chrissy says, "Maybe their rich food has something to do with their colourful feathers by eating hoots loads of fruits." The family is amazed by the beaks as brilliant bonanza bright yellow like a banana! "It's only that our twins alike these brothers try to mimic matrix wings by placing their hand on hips and moving elbows back and double dynamic duo," that was proudly said by Peter. "Ha!" "How cleaver is these playful keen brothers!!!" Chrissy said admirably as she wanted to show off, "Hoot, hoot, and a shout out toot!!" Chrissy was a bit jealous of her younger brothers too!

The lion laid lazily stretching out his loins and showing off his proud prowess pose giving a huge yawn on a grassy lawn. Looking at the lovely lionesses were laying down all about resting further as their addresses were not so flash apart from that lounging lion. The lion's crown head of beard boasts of his large main headdress as a majestic makeover for the lionesses to gaze. The family of huge cats is found stretching their paws over towards the huge lion. Charlie pointed out and said, "Over there is the chosen leader of the family huge cats." "Look at the size of these cats!" Charlie exclaimed. The Lion King that just happened to give a belt of a growl. "Ahhh, wow!" "What a belch he had?" His father observed and said, "How his jaws opened impressively so wide looking scary deep inside all the way as it lifted his neck." "Perhaps his growl called out aloud to the lionesses." "It was his intention to tell those females to come closer over to play by him." Anita expressed and furthermore to say, "What a drama play???" Anita leaned over Peter's way!

"Wow!!" "Have a gander at this beautiful snow leopard!" Said Chrissy. "How lovely to see a snow leopard walking tippy-toe and so very slow." "Look how lovingly it is showing off a rub a dub, do on the side of its body too." "He craves to satisfy a message for sleep time bed bye," Chrissy said. "I bet Snowy can stretch and scratch that itch for you too?" Chrissy nudged her brother Chad! Chad's response to her was surprising. "His kind reminds me of our cat at home, Patty!" "Yeah." Said Chrissy! "How so?" "Really our cat stinks," said Charlie! "Now, now," their mother said, "that is enough of day to insult our Patty in that way!!!"

The tigers are the biggest species of the cat family. Most kinds originate from some countries of Asia and Siberia. They have the loveliest orange black and white patterns on their fur. "This reminds me of our Patty cat which is a tortoiseshell and has loveliest colours too!" Chrissy continues to say. "These young tiger cubs tease and taunt each other as their mother watches by their side." The mother tigress reaches her paw over them. Then she presses her paw to involve in their pulling taunt and tease. "Ghee!" "Let's stay here enjoy watching their interplay all day," Anita said. "Wrestling with the tiger cubs looks like lots of fun," Chrissy said. "As long you both are not caring to carry on pushing at each other, right Chad, not to copy that lingering cat?!" Charlie says, "We are a class wrestling act and we are bad at it." Peter then replied to his sons, "Will you two stop that!" "Oh, please boys cut it out now." "Let's all quickly take a snapshot picture together in with the family of tigers." Peter held the camera and said, "These digital cameras are great as we can see ourselves in the screenshot next to tiger's taunt and play!" "Say tease please!" "Lol" Chrissy said, "Cheese please!"

"Let's take a gander into another den over there, oh Wah!!" "Look onto this side," said Chrissy! Suddenly she felt startled by seeing this slithery snake slides and glides all coiled up its way ascended around and around the tree stump as it has simultaneously sent electricity senses up Chrissy's spine. "Someone say something if you see static hairs rise up even say a snake mention of that?" Chrissy commented, "The ssss, snake python is about 3 meters long and looking dangerous in brown and tan twisted on a stumpy." "Yes!" Says Chad. "So glad it's not an Anaconda so long and farewell for now." "I think I like that snake better to stay beyond that glass stage cage somehow, yeah!!" Sister was happy to step as aside so quietly and feeling so very relieved inside.

"We haven't yet seen the echidna?!" Chrissy asked. "Well, it is also known as a porcupine which comes from Canada."

Then Anita said, "The echidna comes from Australia!" "You guessed it!" "Such an animal small and round which is not going to pick you or pick on me with their quills." "Ouch, yah kidding yah echidna!" Anita said it jokingly and asked, "Hey!" "Does the Echidna move very slowly and very carefully for any reason?" Chrissy mentioned, "Do you see her point?!" She was nodding her head looking at Chad. Their mother moved into an impulsive reaction and reached out to pinch Chad's and Charlie's arms! "Hey, that is not fair to pick on me!" Charlie said. Chad relayed to his mother, "So good excuses mom." "Also, I am glad that you said nothing about the creature from the woodlands such as the skunk!" Chad looked up to his mom!" "Never," Charlie said, "that is just beside my point if anyone could ever get hurt by a skunk?" "Really Charlie and Chad that is plenty enough," Anita said.

"The black and white stripe skunk is a small animal native to North and South America." Chad directed this to Charlie. Their dad Peter said, "Assuming you could adopt her as an interesting pet with the addition to our Patty!?" Peter then looked at Anita and laughed. Then saying, "Although Patty may find it the most remotely affectionate at first glance as it is also smelly and yet it must feel awfully lonely for it to be left on its lonesome!" Charlie disagrees with them. "No not really." Chrissy stepped in and shared her point of view, "I disagree cause our Patty might try to chase it, thinking it was a hairy scary dirty rat?" Chrissy looked at Chad saying, "And maybe her scared encounter with its unique scented odour of a special kind will change her mind assuredly." Charlie remarked, "Who could accuse her of this kind scaredy cat as I believe Patty is an escape artist!" Anita looked at her children shaking off her head feeling a lot of sympathies as she knows her kids love Patty. "Happy now kids?" She remarked

The family walked over to another direction towards a smaller kind of reptile to view a limey green coloured chameleon which was slightly hidden under a leafy coverage of the green tree foliage. It is looking at the twin brothers. Charlie surprised her mother with an expression, "Achoo!!" "Please don't sneeze without covering your nose and excusing yourself." This was Anita's response. Charlie tugged his mother's sleeve. "Watch what this chameleon does now!" The chameleon happened to roll one eye up and then another eye down wildly moving all around!! Chrissy asked, "Is that kind of small animal hunting for bugs??" "Well, well, our green trendy clowns here are bugging me looking dazzled all around my dear." Peter squeezed Anita's arm! Anita said, "The chameleon is particular of changing colours of a bit red flush and a tinge bit blue it is a camouflage of you." Peter continues to say, "It is a chameleon." "We have a very funny trio which any comedian would discover their humorous changeability which anyone might enjoy!" Chad continues to say. "Yes, I am sure." "Take a gander at this lingering reptile while it looks over at our stranger

Chrissy changing too colourfully!" Then Chrissy said, "and our daddy's locks have the same looks!" "Ha, ha, ha!" Charlie said, "I don't get this silliness?" His father said, "Good joke!" "Ah ha," and then he remarked, "Let us put all jokes aside and take a group photo!" Peter was excited and expected to see a colourful chameleon notably next to the family photo! He then reviewed the photo shoot on the camera and said, "Great family portrait next to a tree and a chameleon is a visual of too little to see!" "Wouldn't you agree?" They then walked towards the reptilian group.

A group of crocodiles laying low wallow stuck in the middle pile of margarine mud all huddled about together. "That single crocodile above the rest is staring a beady-eyed with open jaws apart and large teeth aside showed off was its wide grin?" Charlie couldn't take a grasp in and said, "I was feeling rather heavy as a pumpkin," "I will be no way large enough to fit between his teeth with my weight to fit in his chomp," Chad said to Charlie, "Best to break away fast and not any breakfast." "Whoop, whoop, close one!" "That croc snapped his trap shut!" Said Charlie, "Luckily, I am a happy chappy that snappy couldn't catch me in his insides!?"

"Nah, nah, nah, nah, nah," Charlie said as he nudges his brother and pushes Chad along. "Get down low and go, go, go!"

Charlie remarked, "Huh, get some movement happening!" Chrissy sighs and jumped in between their hind knees, "Sorry, I too must break away and not stay for some crunchy party meal!" Chrissy says, "Wow, exactly a whopper snap of a steel trap and his teeth did not terminate me either!" Chrissy in a line stared at the way Chad expressed himself holding out his two long arms and clapped his hands as a stapler machine.

Chrissy says, "Get out of the way Charlie from Chad's long chomps." "He is pretty mean," Chad grinned showing his big smile at her! Charlie laughed, "Ha, ha, ha!!" "I too survived away from his biggest Chad chomps!!" Said Chrissy.

"Hurry!" "Come quickly!" "Coming soon!" We heard the voice from around the corner. The trainer's voice was heard from afar off. Chrissy was thinking it might be a circus about to start in ZOOFARI?

"Snack time?" "Showtime?" Then Chrissy smiles and thinks it's awesome,

"Comedy show comes to town!" Chrissy looking at her younger brother Charlie!

"Look out all you happy campers," the Zookeeper said. "Around the next corner zoo show time start at noontime."

"Happy campers hurry quickly." The young Charlie raised his voice expressively, very clearly and excitedly. Anita was feeling petrified at the young Charlie's screaming voice!

The mother directed her voice to Charlie, "Was that another wild animal noise I just heard from you, young man?" "Thankfully, you can keep the noise down!" Anita nudged him forward. Charlie whispered, "yah, bah, da, bah, I feel so happy too!" Charlie continued to raise his voice.

"Let us all scream out happy chap, ice-cream and popcorn very quick snap!" Chrissy bumped Charlie saying, "Let us all go forwards to the show and leave chomps behind!"

"Hooray count me in as well!" Chad shouted too!

Peter quickly took hold of his son's hands as Anita suddenly said, "If only it was going to be that easy, right?" She was looking at Peter and then at them. Chad was copying signs and sounds of Charlie's wild animal like expressions. Their mother directed the sharp sound of her voice towards the boys. "Not another peep from both of you." "You get a great big idea?" Seeing mom's eyes said it all.

The zookeepers usher the crowds to take their seats happily for the anticipation of an animal show.

"Good afternoon folks!" "It's a good show and Welcome everybody." "My name is Grant," the zookeeper shouted over the speaker. "Snack time?" "Showtime, anyone for ice-cream and popcorn now!" "Let's give a big cheer out for the stars of our show!!"

Grant was over at the grandstand. The crowds all clapped and cheered very excitedly!!!

Suddenly Cassidy, the gray, blue and white crested falcon swooped over yonder way down low over the crowds ducking heads! The Falcon wowed the crowds! Bill their trainer enters the stage with a leathery glove covered his left hand and his arm afar stretched out.

Cassidy carefully flew with his wings spread out over heading all the crowd to the other side landing on a perch.

The trainer took hold of the falcon and it rested on his hand. "Hi, folks and welcome all!" I am Bill and here is the ever so swiftly, nifty Cassidy." Bill explained that "Cassidy is a young 2 years old Falcon one of sixty species of diurnal birds of prey from the order of Falconiformes." "Cassidy has keen eyesight which he uses to hunt for his prey." "Please welcome into our arena the wonderful Cassidy." The crowds give a cheer which brought a wonderful atmosphere. "I would like to give a member from the audience the opportunity to stand up and participate in an exercise with Cassidy!" "Can anyone in this crowd please stand up to show us a cash note and hold it up in the air," Bill asked. Anita stood upholding a $5 note. Bill asked, "May we know your name, please?" "Anita," she said. Bill said,

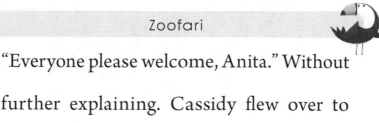

"Everyone please welcome, Anita." Without further explaining. Cassidy flew over to Anita and took from her hand a rolled-up $5 note. She thought to herself, oh my what an idea. Then Cassidy clasped the cash note into his claws as he quickly flew over the crowds towards the trainer. Bill exclaimed, "What a hoot the falcon took your loot!!!" "Well done Cassidy!" "Thank you, Anita, for the cash tip." "How lovely is Cassidy?" "No need to run Miss," Bill exclaimed. Chrissy said, "Oooh, wow!" "Now watch as Cassidy will return the money." "Yes, is that right!" Bill said knowingly, "Honesty is always the best policy!" Said Bill. Cassidy clasped the

$5 note and returned the cash note to Anita. Bill said to her, "Thank you Anita for your participation!" Cassidy flew over to Bill and landed safely. Anita stood up and clapped her hands along with all the crowd who all cheered for Cassidy! Bill then introduced the following, "Welcome to our next act coming into our arena!" Bill continued to charm the crowds!

"Around the corner comes Lisa-Lee! "Hooray!" Says Bill! Everyone claps, as the two caretakers held hands with Lisa-Lee! The trainers introduced their act, "Welcome, our orangutan, Lisa-Lee!" "She is three years old orangutan ape all the way from the rain forests of Borneo, Malaysia."

"She is one of the families of five staying with us at ZOOFARI." Bill says, "Lisa-lee is wearing an orange, pink and white polka dot tutu!" "How do you do Lisa-Lee?" Lisa-Lee stuck out her tongue at Bill, Bill said, "Well now," "Welcome, Lisa-Lee's trainers Lila and Layla." Lisa-Lee claps her hands lifting them up above showing off to all her audience. The crowds also followed clapping their hands to give her the warmest welcome!!! "I am Lila and my colleague trainer here is Layla!" "We are Lisa-Lee's trainers and you guessed it right, we are soul sisters too," "Ok folks!" Layla says, "Look on folks and welcome the ever so beautiful, lovely Lisa-Lee who will be happiest performing for you?" Lila says, "Lisa-Lee sits, she meditates and takes after her primate relatives within the zoo, ha, ha." "Really I am kidding!" "Actually, Lisa-Lee is a special primate and demonstrates strumming her lips with her fingers and combing her hair lightly!" Lila continued saying, "She likes showing off her long legs!"

"Shocked, aren't you too?" She was looking at Layla and Lisa-Lee's responses as they nodded. Layla then places a pink helmet over Lisa-Lee's head, then Lisa-Lee is grinning widely showing off all her teeth. Layla smiles, "She is showing off her party looks." Said Layla. "Lisa-Lee is showing off her hips swinging side to side," She is an active, attractive female orangutan all the way from Malaysia and she loves to entertain our folks." "Of course, she can hula hoop swing off loops." Said Lila. Crowds go wild while she is swinging off the hula hoops. They love her. Lisa-Lee then goes for the swing as she stood up holding onto the swing and holding onto the chains as she swung the swing herself. Lisa-Lee waited for Lila to push her further and higher as she was swinging back and forwards, Lisa-Lee was also shouting, "Ou, Ou, Ou!" Then the trainer Layla encourages her by calling out to Lisa-Lee to come over towards the round circuit route. Lila calls out, "Lisa-Lee, let's show the crowds your favourite stunning stunt." "She naturally jumps onto the huge skateboard and now she will show us off a trick or two!!"

Whizzing over on the ramp as she pushes herself to gain speed and over the bumps as she goes. Lila says, "She is not that shy gal not at all." "She has no excuses for showing up not late for her date!" Lila the trainer extends her arm to show off Lisa-Lee. The crowds clapping their hands and wowed by her stunts. "Watch now folks", "Lisa-Lee tilts the board about as she roars into a

spin, BRRRRRR!" "How about that folks,
hardy har, har!" Then she gets back onto the
ramp! These kids love her and think she is
a great class act!! "Ghee, what a show-off as
she turns into a bright orange glow show
wouldn't you know!" Grant said as he jumps
into the scene, "Give a hearty thanks to the
adorable Lisa-Lee and both her beautiful
orangutan trainers Lila and Layla too," the
trainers bowed with Lisa-Lee holding onto
her hands! Crowds all clap cheerfully! Peter
whispered to Anita. "If it was only that easy,
right?" "I feel like going for tango or for a
skateboard?" Peter said, "Gorgeous, I was
taken by this rolling about the awesome act."

He felt to express his feelings towards her by blowing a kiss. "I guess not quite like the flamingos?!!" Anita said. "orangutan charm flowing acts go into a whirl of tutu twirl, oh my word!!" Peter then chuckled and clapped his hands along with Anita!!! She said, "How wonderful!"

Grant is on side stage giving a commentary about a 2 years old baby gray elephant named Harry! Grant states that Harry is a member of the family of African elephants in ZOOFARI. "Will all the crowds please clap to welcome Harry and carry on encouraging him!" The audience is watching a baby elephant spraying out water from his trunk next to the zookeeper! Grant says, "It's simply a hot day to go about to play and I need to cool off this way!!" "Welcome folks, Harry the baby elephant is thrilled to perform for us." "He is happily flapping his jumbo ears." Grant shows him little prompts, "Harry continues with his little stomps and perhaps his head is not too drunk to play a soccer game, right there?" Grant continues commenting,

Harry had some water from the trough and sprayed water over Grant again. "Lol" "Harry's family are expecting him to return soon to his mother in the stables so without further due folks." "Here is Harry ready as ever for a baby show of our all-time favourites." Crowds are clapping! "He will run and shoot out with the soccer ball!!" Harry is flapping his little jumbo ears eagerly waiting for a fun play. "He is looking ever so cute wearing a white frilly collar over his neck as part of his uniform playoff!" Unexpectedly, Grant rolls out a jumbo white and black soccer ball as big as Harry. Harry comes running for the play, he is ready as ever to bunt the ball. Crowds watch as it rolls across the sandy court. "Harry hobbles as he swings his head side to side bunting the oversized soccer ball!"

"What super trooper folks." "The soccer player gets the ball between the goal post; don't you agree folks?" "Not a worry as he had plenty of practices!" Harry swings his trunk up facing the brunt of the ball and it runs far off down outside the net! "Please don't frown Harry did not skip town!" "He, he, he," Grant said jokingly! The crowds watch that soccer ball skipped, slid out, and missed the goal post and the ball continues to roll outside the post. Crowds voices raised in an outcry "Arrr, ahhhhh, ohhhh, Harry!" He tries for another attempt. Grant calls out to the crowds, "Let's get full control Harry!" "It doesn't surprise me as Harry attempts for a 2nd play, here we go!" "Oh, oh, oh, Olay, Olay, Olay!!" With a surprise backgrounder sound of trumpet blurb! Tah, Rah, Rah! Grant positions the ball in the field! "Wow watch Harry's determination and actions of pumping those swinging pouncing little legs forcibly about for the ball." All out with powerful bunt from his front snout pushing the ball forwards and out. "Harry's motion of sprints running for the play of fun in the field rolling onwards all the way, makes me want to say Hooray!" "He is shooting for the ball out again for good luck." "What a gorgeous baby elephant running for the play of his super bowl win." "Come folks to cheer him on again." Grant encourages the crowds with them, "Come on Harry!" Harry wonderfully bunts the ball for the net and scores a goal. "Well done Harry!" Charlie yells out, "Wow whee, there's no place else I'd rather be!" Charlie swings a fist in the air!!

"Hooray for Harry!!!" Grant shouts a good cheer out!

"A round of applause folks, please!" Harry's baby steps flowed as tip, tap, toe along he goes standing on three legs. Then one back bent leg out far as he watched Grant pointing his one leg back out for his cue. Harry's pointer trunk went straight out to face the net!

Harry displayed a confident winning stature! Grant says, "Is statue Harry, of winning poise?"

"Now that is so cool and very showy of you!" Grant said.

The crowds all cheer out clapping their hands.

"Yeah..... how unbelievable!" "What a wonderful play of the day!" Grant shouts out!

Many people were snapping photos!

Harry returns to the trough for water to swings his trunk up over then sprays water onto Grant all over again! Everyone was clapping their hands and laughing. Grant said, "Easy Harry!"

Crowds laughed happily, "He got the play and scored a winning point for today!"

"Now for our next act, this is pretty GIGI." Grant shows the audience coming onto the stage from the left. "Here comes the wonderful trainer Paula with her pink cowboy boots." Paula thanks Grant for the introduction! Paula calls out

"Welcome to all, you are all in for a big treat." She continues to say, "Now please don't look at me!" "Here comes Pretty GIGI?" "It is a fashion show?" Paula says. Chrissy continues to whisper to her mother, "What next I wonder?"

"Here is Gigi with her favourite pink feathery Cowboy hat with her pink and purple vest on!" and gallops to appease the crowds. Paula encourages the crowds, "Let's all welcome Gigi!" Paula was clapping. Chrissy is watching a young zebra galloping over a bridge. Chrissy watches on diligently! Gigi trots a lot and she galloped over a little bridge! Trainer shouts out. "Go right ahead!" "Did you see that folks it's a zebra crossing, he, he, he!" "Gigi just cleared the crossing over the bridge!" "Let's all clap hands and encourage her!" "Gigi, isn't she a lot of fun folks?!!!" "Kids we will now sing a nursery rhyme." "So, kids following after me once I

signal to lift my arm only then, Ring- a-Ring
o' Rosies,"

Paula calls Gigi to come towards her. Gigi
gains her speed to circle around Paula and
she gains momentum then jumps through
a big hoop and again. Paula says, "Gigi runs
Rings around the Posey hoops," Paula holds
up a pocket full of posies!! Paula sings a
nursery rhyme, "Ring-a-Ring o' Rosies." "A
pocket full of posies." Paula singing, "Please
kids you all stand up now." "Kids then you
all can hunch down!!" Thanks kids as they
laugh. Paula tossed all the posies up in the
air for Gigi to jump through the poesy hoops
and Rosie petals fell all over the ground. The

kids were so happily laughing!! "Thank you, all kids, applauding for Gigi's fun tricks." Gigi continues to run rings around the green bushes. Paula says, "Gigi does not mind a quick hind kick every time to show off her sweet tricks." "Gigi enjoys all the quick tricks." Paula is cheering for Gigi and Grant is smiling. "That concludes the end of this show!" "Oh Gigi, do one more trick as I don't deny she so talented," Grant said. As Chrissy sighed and she quickly replied by saying, "Gigi is the best, oh what fun and so cute, yah!"

Paula signals Gigi to do the finale stunt!

Gigi kneeled on her two front knees. Grant states out loud, "Gigi is such a clever talent let's show our gratitude for Paula and Gigi's performance today!"

All crowds clapping and standing up. "What really good Shooooow!" Paula exclaimed!!

"Now for the next Act over to our right platform." Grant pointing over to his right side by the water pool area. "Let's all welcome Chester the seal." "Wonder what the noise is all about?" Grant shouting on the speaker system.

"Rat, ta tat, tat, ra ta tat, tat!!!"

2222222222

"Welcome Chester" Grant exclaimed. "I, Grant am Chester's trainer." "Chester is pushing a car by his nose on stage with loopy wobbly wheels." Grant started to explain, "This incredible car could not give a lift for any passenger on board stage." "Ahhh, well." Shrugged his shoulders! "Chester" "Arhhhh, Ulp," as Chester is looking for friends to receive a seal of approval. "Welcome again Chester!" "Our well-loved Chester." Grant said, "This lovely Harbour Seal has capabilities to make many different sounds." "He was found from the Northern Hemisphere." Seals have footed fins which enables them to stay on land for long periods

72

of time. "Chester is a lot of fun to be with."

Chester's trainer Grant takes a mini size set bongo drums in his hands. "Can Chester play the drums too?" Grant exclaimed! Grant was taken by surprise whilst showing Chester those small drums. Chester leaned over and kissed Grant on the cheek. Grant said, "Mr. Googles." "I meant to say, Chester!" "I lost my train of thought." The audience applause.

"Look about?" "Look by the side is a bigger set of huge tight drums for his particular size a spectacular sound!" Chester climbed up the three steps platform. Chester's flipper taps on the top of a beat thump thump, thump, thump, thump.

Chester laughs, "Ump, ulp, ulp,"

Then Chester gulped down some fish that Grant tossed over to him. Grant lifts his arms up with a Huge toothbrush. "Heavy!"

"What's so fishy a tasty dishy?!" Grant says. "After all, he must brush between each meal of breakfast and lunch." Grant motions as he tries to brush Chester's teeth.

Then Chester nods his head up and down in the agreement and gives a big sigh!! "Aargh, Aargh!!" "How lovely is Chester." "Oh, my dear?"

Grants say, "A little smelly though for you, any chance there is more for me??"

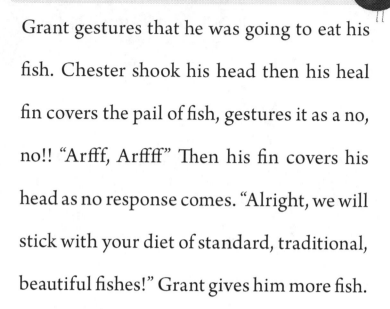

Grant gestures that he was going to eat his fish. Chester shook his head then his heal fin covers the pail of fish, gestures it as a no, no!! "Arfff, Arffff" Then his fin covers his head as no response comes. "Alright, we will stick with your diet of standard, traditional, beautiful fishes!" Grant gives him more fish.

The crowds love it and clapping their hands! Grant pulls out a huge bushy moustache from his pocket and places it over Chester's nose for a quick show.

"Is Chester really a Walrus folks?!" "What are we going to do about it?" "I had to shave it off before the show as it would help him with his balancing Act!!" "Love it, just kidding folks," Grant holds a big colourful balloon ball to balance on Chester's nose. "Well done, Chester!" he is balancing the ball on his nose. Then with his nose tossed the ball back over to Grant! Chester now is balancing on his front fins and hind fins stand back up poise. Then Grant seizes to place a small tennis ball upon his nose. Chester is encouraged to bounce the ball upon his nose. Grant remarks over the loudspeaker, "Chester's diet is so balanced that he eats 4 pails of fish a day." Grant holds the tennis ball and then throws a fish for Chester to catch.

"Oh, he has caught a specialty big fish and he is looking dapper in a pretty striped bow." Chester stands over his fins on top of the platform step and waves with his heals then stands down. Chester shows off while he claps with his front fins over the side of the platform stand. Crowds gave mighty cheer!! Chester then throws a kiss to give his seal of affection. "Wooshhh." "Terrific Chester power move of a gesture!!" Grant shouted!

Chester nods his head up and down. Grant signals Chester. "Thank you very much, Chester" as Chester slides off stage. The Crowds are clapping.

"Well what's next?" "Where is Waldo?",
Grant looks over towards Roger, Waldo's
trainer. "Welcome Roger the trainer," Roger
then introduces his act!

"We are happy to introduce the Walrus
Waldo," Roger exclaimed happily!

Crowds applause. "Waldo is a very
handsome walrus!" "No sir it's not Chester's
cousin but our trusty Walrus!" "How do you
find Waldo?" "He is not hard to miss because
he weighs over 300 kilos!" "Roger says, "He
is the biggest and best buddy ever!"

Waldo appears a bit shy looking up into
the sky then covering his face with his fin!
"Perhaps he has forgotten to put on his

suntan oil?" Roger replied. Waldo looks up and receives some fish.

"How do you find Waldo?" Roger asks Grant. Grant replies, "His looks are fresh, fun, and friendly!" "Easy Tiger" as Waldo grunts a noise! "UURRGGHH, Huh", Roger raises his voice, "I am Roger, Waldo's trainer and today Waldo is going to perform his biggest act to climb up the ramp and flip off the plank diving into the water!!" Roger continues by swinging his arm upwards pointing towards the plank. Waldo lifts his fin looking up at the plank then looks back at Roger nosing an action of an unforgettable no. Roger continues, "Yes," nodding his head, "Ladies and gentlemen he will climb up the 3 meters high ramp then approach the plank!" Roger says to Waldo, "Oh my word it's not going to be me Waldo that will go all the way there to the top." Waldo looks at Roger's hand movement action up to the plank. "Is that right Waldo?" Waldo repeated his look up then way over at Roger and back up onto that plank!" Waldo says, "Waargh!" Roger says, "The security taking on a tea break now!" "Stay looking very busy now by hiking on a trail, thank goodness."

Waldo looks away gestures as he is looking out for them. Then he lays flat-lying low! Roger nods and says, "Come now, looking good with teatime, Waldo!"

"Repeat all after me, folks, let us go, Waldo!"

Roger says, "Let's go for a swim Waldo!" All were cheering on Waldo! "Waldo, Waldo!" Waldo was looking a bit pale and nodding at that pail of amazing little fishes! Roger gave Waldo some fish, "Good Waldo.!" "He knows it's a big dive off that plank!" Roger says, "I will sit with the audience while you go up there alone!" Waldo sounds a big, "Arrh, Argh!!" Of approval! "Ok, I am not that artful dodger as it seems!" The audience sounds, "Oh, Ahhh!!" "Cheer up folks and look here!" Roger opens his long raincoat......and pulls out a long rubber fish and shows it off to Waldo! "Seize your huge prize!!" The audience all started laughing! "Ruff, Ruff, Ruff!" Waldo barked and showed off, he showed his nodding. Roger said, "How delicately and deliciously he has put it!" "Amazing Waldo," Roger gives him some more fish. "What potential." Roger encourages Waldo to follow him as he and Waldo mimic the waddle walk. Waldo is following Roger going up to the rise of the challenge towards the ramp and showing off that huge fish! Roger looks back and Waldo also looks back. Roger nods his head and Waldo also nods. "Waldo is following

Roger Dodger." "That's GREAT!" Roger said loudly.

Waldo stays so close to him watching him holding the big fish. "You made it Waldo" said Roger! Now as Roger looks down into the water. Roger says to all the audience,

"How do you find Waldo?"

"I often ask this," said Roger. "Very handsome Waldo!" "Let's give Waldo another applause folk!!" A little nipper in the audience yelled out, "Don't do it Waldo!" Roger said, "But Noooo!" "Waldo can do it, it's very easy!" Waldo belched out an, "Arrrrrrrhg." A growl came. Roger jumped forwards to the plank. Roger had a startled jump up high near the plank. "Waldo you startled me." "Folks, Waldo is such a tease!" "Waldo!" Roger says, "I was planning to play golf outdoors but I chose to be next to Waldo's big course!" "Isn't this true?" "Waldo is the ever so lovely, fresh, fun, and friendly Walrus as usual", Roger said loudly so the audience could hear it! Waldo showed his head held high, "Ruff, Ruff, and Ruff", and nodded with resilience! He then was given some more small fish. Waldo gives up a sexy whistle. "Woot, Whoooooo" "Sexy whistle, perfect, good folks!" The audience then applauded Waldo. Waldo was also appeasing with applause. "What really good

Shooooow!" "Roger that!" another growl, "Arrrrrrrrgh." "Folks, truly Waldo is a super, duper trooper!" "We love!!!" Roger gestures the forward signal.

Waldo swooshes forwards along with the springboard as he went far off the plank with his weight bounced off. Waldo flipped up and out into the air as a spin of spectacular! People had their eyes glued upon Waldo! Waldo splashed into the water. Gigantic Splash! Splash of water covered all people in the front two rows. Roger yelled out, "Oh, folks what a big wave!" Roger continues forwards while he returns to the platform to gives the signal of the waving hand! "Amazing Waldo!" "Give an applause folks" "Well done!" Waldo got the signal to lift his fin to wave at the audience. Waldo continued to swim along with one fin in the air as though a shark was in the pool. "Oh, nice one, Waldo!" He returned close to the water edge gliding towards the platform. He swooshes up onto the step platform holding himself onto his fins. He returned for a bit more of Roger's tanker tease! Roger holds up the big fish and says, "Well done, perfect!" "May the force be with you!!" "Well done, well done Waldo you put the audience onto their heals!" "What a great showstopper!!" The audience all cheered and applauded.

Waldo groans, "Arf! Arf! Arf!" Roger says to them, "Aaaaafter all folks it was a flipping wonderful show I have ever seen!!!" Then they both bowed to appease the crowds.

Then Grant the Zookeeper says, "On behalf of all the trainers and animals at ZOOFARI please feel welcome to ask any questions." "Otherwise thank you all very much for coming and that's the end of our finest show!" "It is a funny, sunny, spectacular day and I hope you all enjoyed our company which was lots of fun." "Thanks again for the visit to ZOOFARI." The audience all clapping loudly.

As the family exited the show. They all had felt a nifty warm glow. It really was a fine show. Peter showing off his expression towards his family with a gasp," I worked up all of our appetites together after such an animal show as this." "It's the best welcome and closing of a show I'd ever seen." "Let's all stopover at the canteen!" The children were agreeing with their dad as they were smiling. Peter says, "Later on if we are not too tired, we'll journey the rest of our way to see other animals of ZOOFARI Kingdom." "Really we had such a remarkable and so far, a memorable day." Anita said, "We truly enjoyed ourselves today!" "Which animals at the zoo are your favourite most of all?"

Anita asked the children. "Take a guess

which animal personally was my choice

and why would I naturally choose that one?"

The family was carried away by their huge

playful day!!

Printed in the United States
By Bookmasters